K.C.
FACES PEER PRESSURE

Written by Gerald Lee, II
Illustrated by Patrick Carlson

Dedication

To my daughters Danielle, Denice, Dominique and Giana; your mother and I are so proud of you and what you have already done in a short time. We look forward to ultimately seeing who God will mold you to be and are glad to play a part in your development. We love you all!

Daddy

Sonnyville! There are many things to do and places to go. It is a place full of enjoyment, excitement, and is known for its peaceful environment. Living in Sonnyville is a young man named K.C. He is a good kid and normally tries to do what is right. One Saturday morning, K.C. woke up and wanted to do something fun and different.

"No video games or T.V. for me today! I want to do something healthy and fun," said K.C. So, he decided the park would be a great place for exercise and, of course, some fun. But everyone knows going to the park by yourself is not fun, so he decided to invite a friend to come along. "Who should I invite?" thought K.C. He had been trying to find true friends who do good things. "Everyone will not always be my true friend, so I really have to be careful who I spend my time with," thought K.C.

He thought about it for a while, and the only person he could think of was his childhood friend Tyler. Tyler and K.C. had been friends since they were in first grade. They often had the same teacher and grew up playing outdoors together when their homework and house chores were finished. Tyler was a lot of fun! He was an exciting little boy that loved all kinds of sports and competition. Even though he was a good kid, he sometimes got into trouble because he liked to take risks and did not always think about the consequences before he did things. "Let's have fun!" is what he would shout and is exactly what he did.

K.C. called Tyler and with excitement in his voice said, "Hey Tyler, want to go to the park?" "K.C!" shouted Tyler, "it should be cool, let me just ask my mom!" His mother told him after he finished his Saturday morning chores, he was free to go with his friend.

He called K.C. back and told him, "I'll be there in thirty minutes!"
"Sounds good to me, see you then!" said K.C. As K.C got ready to leave,
his little sister stopped him and asked where he was going. They had a
good relationship but hanging out with a little sister is not always cool.

"I'm going to the park Danielle and, no, you cannot come this time." He waited on her to shout, "I'm telling mom!" or even start to cry. Instead, she did something a little different this time. She simply frowned and looked very, very sad. When K.C. saw this, there was only one thing he could say. "Ok, you can come, just don't give me that look anymore."

Quickly her face lit up with a smile and K.C. realized that it is important not just to spend time with your friends, but your family too. As they walked up the street, Danielle started telling K.C. how much she loved the park and how the swings and merry-go-round are her favorite!

As they got to the park, Tyler was already there and shouted, "hey guys!" K.C. and Danielle both said "hi" and then K.C. added, "so, what should we do?" Tyler and Danielle looked at each other like it was a race to come up with something the fastest. Before Tyler could think of anything, Danielle yelled "swings!" "Ok Danielle, you got it! But not too long because last time your stomach started hurting when you swung too high," said K.C.

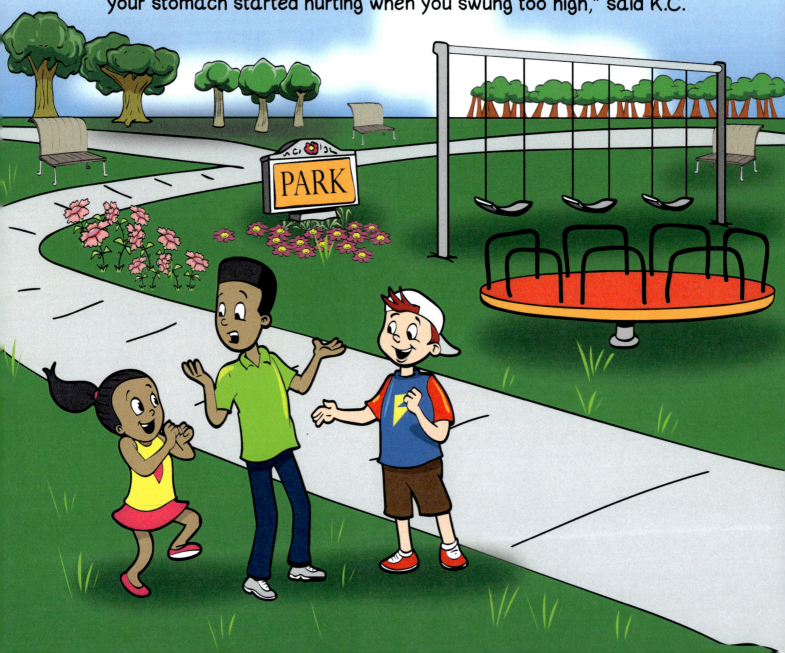

As Tyler listened to their conversation, he let it be known that for him, taking the risk of being sick was ok, as long as he had some fun! Thinking like this is what sometimes got him in trouble. As they walked to the swings, they noticed a little girl sitting all by herself.

"We should ask her to come play with us K.C., she's all by herself!" said Danielle. K.C. thought for a moment and then felt it would be a great idea! So, he asked Tyler what he thought, and Tyler saw it as a chance to make a new friend. Tyler gave a big thumbs up.

When they got to the little girl, K.C. introduced everyone. "This is Danielle, Tyler, and I'm K.C." In the same friendly voice, he then asked, "what's your name?" the little girl looked surprised because she had been playing at the park for weeks, and no one had ever said anything to her. "Hola, my name is Cristina and I just moved here two months ago," she said. "I think moving is cool. You get to see new places and make new friends," said Tyler. Cristina did not see it the same though. "That is true sometimes Tyler, but it may take a long time to find friends and start to fit in," said Cristina.

K.C. said with confidence, "well as long as you're here, we will be your friends!" Cristina looked very happy and felt good that someone cared about her feelings and wanted to be her friend. Danielle added, "we were just on our way to the swings, would you like to come?" "I sure would!" said Cristina.

As they walked to the swing set, they all noticed there was an envelope sticking out of the dirt, under one of the swings. K.C. picked up the envelope, and to all their surprise, it had 40 dollars inside of it. While they all stood there wondering what they could do with the money, Cristina said, "hey, why don't we each take ten dollars." Since there was now four of them, she felt an even split would be fair.

Each of them felt like they were rich and started thinking about what they could do with their money. Danielle thought about a teddy bear while Tyler thought about a new basketball. Cristina thought about candy and K.C. thought about a cheeseburger and fries!

At this point, there was only one thing left to do - split the money! Everyone looked at K.C. and waited for him to give them each their share of the money. Just as K.C. was about to give them their ten dollars, he asked "wait...the money may have belonged to someone else and what if they were looking for it right now?"

"Well, I'm sure by now they don't need it. Besides, we found it, so it belongs to us now. Right, Tyler?" asked Cristina. Tyler looked a little confused and said, "K.C, we did find the money just like Cristina said, so that does make it ours." Danielle even said, "K.C. no one else is here to claim the money so we should go ahead and keep it." They all looked at K.C. with a serious stare.

K.C. thought about everything they were saying to him. He knew his sister and friends wanted something and he was in the perfect position to give it to them and make them happy. But he also knew that taking the money could be stealing. "What do I do?" He said to himself and he began to sweat.

After careful consideration, K.C. decided to do the right thing. K.C. looked at all of his friends and boldly asked, "what if that money was yours and you lost it?" How would you feel if someone had the chance to return it, but chose not to so they could get something?" With frowns on their faces, he let them know it is easy to keep the money, but the right thing to do is turn it in.

K.C. then looked for the first adult he could find at the park and when he found one, he explained to her that he and some friends found some money and would like to return it. "Oh, thank you young man!" said the lady in an excited voice. She then said, "I have been here all day long looking for this. It is my daughter's birthday money!"

All of the kids soon felt really good because K.C. stood for what was right and they all thanked him for making the best choice. As K.C. and Danielle walked home, she patted her brother on the back and said, "I'm proud of you, big brother! Really, really proud!"

Practical Life Lessons

1. Video games and T.V. is fun but getting out and being active is better for your health.

2. You have to be careful how you pick your friends because everyone you meet does not always want what is best for you.

3. True friends are hard to find so when you find one, treat them right and hold on to the friendship.

4. It is ok to have fun and try new things, but you should always think about the danger before you do it.

5. Going outside to play is important, but it is even more important to finish your chores before you play.

6. Spending time with friends is something you normally want to do; but spending time with your family is something you need to do.

7. You sometimes think people will try to get you in trouble if you are not being nice but sometimes, you just hurt their feelings really badly.

8. Being considerate of other people's feelings can really make the difference in someone's life.

9. Many times, when you handle your business right the first time, it will free up even more time for fun!

10. You sometimes talk to the same people over and over because you know them, but do not be afraid to meet new people. It may be your next close friend.

11. It is very easy to think of fun things to do with someone else's belongings, but you should always try to give it back to the right person.

12. Peer pressure is never fun. In fact, it can be very hard to deal with. If your friends do this, do your best to stay calm and think about what is right.

13. When you have decisions to make, it is a good idea to think of someone who has already overcome challenges.

14. Do not be afraid to say how you feel and explain why you feel that way, and always have a good attitude.

15. When you make the right decisions, it could become someone else's blessing because of it.

16. You never know who is watching what you do or how you help others make the right decisions. When you do the right thing, you make others proud, but most of all, you can be proud of yourself!

Made in the USA
Coppell, TX
15 April 2020